ONE DAY, THE END

Short, Very Short, Shorter-than-Ever Stories

REBECCA KAI DOTLICH Illustrated by **FRED KOEHLER**

BOYDS MILLS PRESS

AN IMPRINT OF HIGHLIGHTS

Honesdale, Pennsylvania

Boyds Mills Press
An Imprint of Highlights
815 Church Street
Honesdale, Pennsylvania 18431
Printed in Malaysia

ISBN: 978-1-62091-451-9
Library of Congress Control Number: 2014958544
First edition
Production by Sue Cole
The text of this book is set in Popstar Autograph
and Rather Loud.
The drawings are done digitally.
10 9 8 7 6 5 4 3 2 1

For all young writers who imagine and create
    their own middles
and with special thanks to Ian, who laughed,
and writer pal Lola Schaefer who, one day,
    spotted the promise. The end.

—RKD

For Quail, who takes me stomping

—FK

For every **STORY** there is a **BEGINNING** and an **END,** but what happens **IN BETWEEN** makes **ALL** the **DIFFERENCE.**

One day... I WENT TO SCHOOL.

I CAME HOME

The End

One day...

HIM! The End

HE FOUND ME. The End

I gave it to
MOM.

ONE DAY... I RAN AWAY.

One day... I WANTED TO BE A

I
W
A
S
.

The End

ONE DAY...

I felt like **STOMPING**.

ONE DAY... I TOOK

A BATH.

SO DID

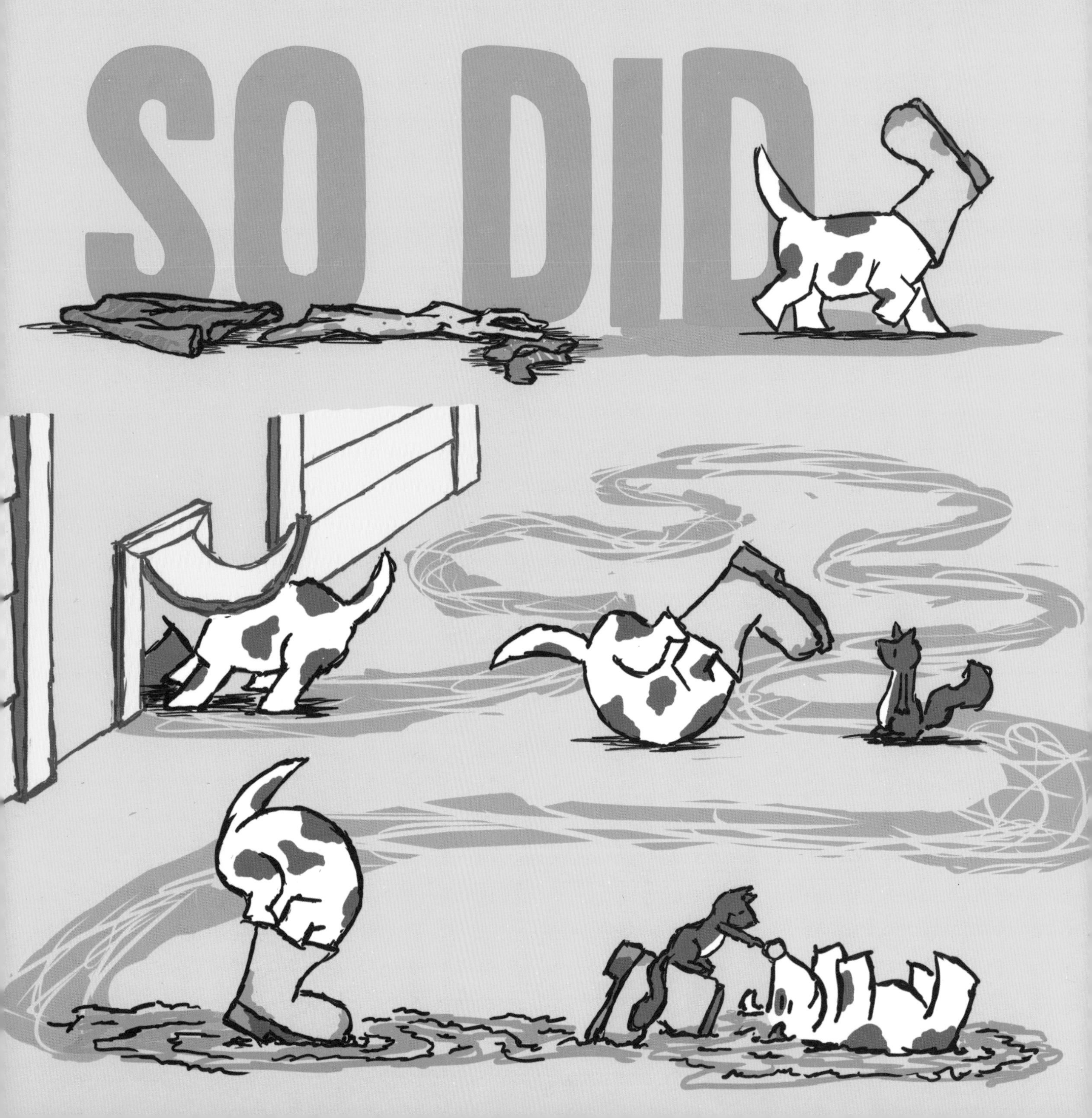

MY DOG.

The End